This book belongs to

....

Written by Sarah Creese.
Illustrated by Lara Ede.

Sparkle Town Fairies

Susie the Sapphire Fairy

and the Glitter Games

Sarah Creese * Lara Ede

make believe ideas

In **Sparkle Town**, among the fields,
beside a shimmering pool,
there stood a bright blue building:
the **Sapphire Riding School!**

RIDING SCHOOL

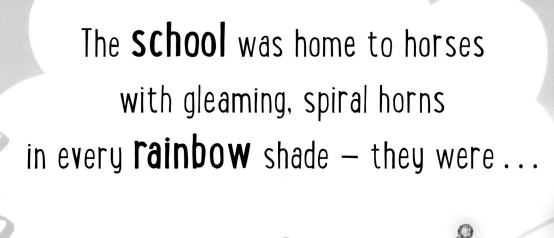

The **school** was home to horses
with gleaming, spiral horns
in every **rainbow** shade — they were . . .

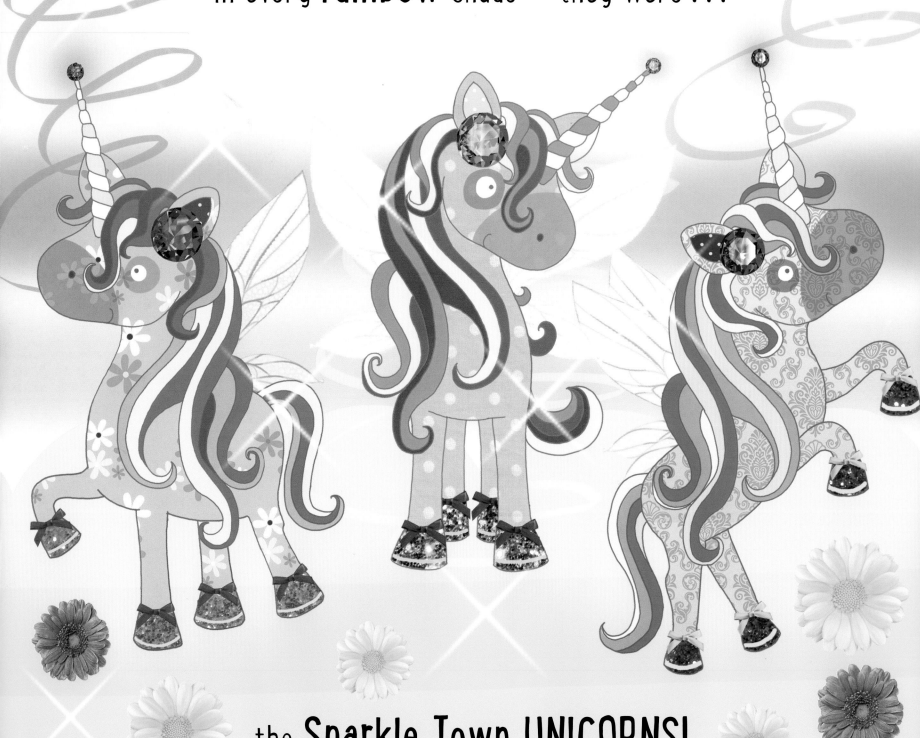

the **Sparkle Town UNICORNS!**

Susie the Sapphire Fairy

was in charge of sports and games.

She cared for all the unicorns
and knew each one by name.

With her glittering, **sapphire wand**, Susie would invent

sparkling balls,

Whooooosh

and **nets,**

Swish
Swish

and **sticks**

Whizzzzz

for **any** sports event!

Susie **loved** all kinds of sports,
but best of all, by far,
was Fairy Land's great **Glitter Games** –
creator of **SUPERSTARS**.

SPARKLE TOWN
PRESENTS

Sparkle Town were this year's hosts,
so Susie **HAD** to win.
She said, "I'm sure we'll beat them all.
Let training time begin!"

THE GLITTER GAMES

The fairies trained hard every day,
and Susie took the **lead**.

"Not like that, like this!" she groaned.

"Now try again — with **SPEED!**"

This went on for hours and hours
'til Daphne said, "Let's rest."
But Susie cried, "No time to stop –
we have to be the best!"

Can't we rest now?

Fed up with being told what to do
and Susie's tough regime,

the fairies said, "We've had enough!
We want you OFF the team."

SUSIE FUMED! Her cheeks turned red.
She stomped off with a HUMPH
and wouldn't talk to anyone –
she truly had the grumps.

Good job, Team!

With **Susie gone,** the team trained on through rain and windy weather. And Susie saw that **without her**... they worked better together.

Hmm, maybe I was wrong.

At last the **GLITTER GAMES** began!
The fairies were prepared.

Over here!

They **won** the first round, then the next —
no other team compared!

Got it.

They made it to the **final match**,
and here, their biggest threat:

Team Glitter
is the best!

the **Glitter City fairy team** –
their toughest rivals yet.

The fairies tried; they **whizzed** and **charged**
but couldn't get ahead.

The Glitters
are too good!

At halftime they felt tired and down.
"We're losing!" Rosie said.

And then **DISASTER** truly struck when Daphne **tripped** and fell!

"Time out!" shouted the referee.

"Team Talk!" Rosie yelled.

Not so sparkly now, are we.

Meanwhile, Susie **watched**, wide-eyed, and despite how cross she felt, seeing her friends in trouble just made her want to **help**.

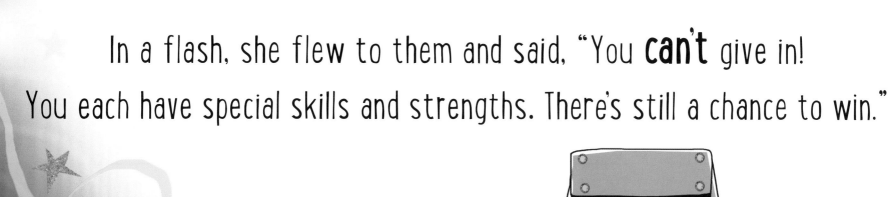

In a flash, she flew to them and said, "You **can't** give in! You each have special skills and strengths. There's still a chance to win."

"Rosie, you're good in defense; the rest of you, attack!
I could fill in Daphne's place – if you'll have me back."

They nodded and smiled at Susie:
"Let's give this plan a try!"
With Susie by their side again,
they **flew** into the sky.

The fairies tried their very best:
they listened and worked as one.
But the **Glitters** were still better,
and in the end … **THEY** won.

SPARKLE TOWN	GLITTER CITY
11	14

WINNER ★ GLITTER CITY ★ WINNER

Susie **frowned**. "I let you down.
I know now I was mean
when I didn't listen in training
or work well with the team.
You're better off **without me**."
She looked down at her feet . . .

"Don't be silly," the fairies said.
"You make our team COMPLETE!"

We need you, Susie!

Back at the school, Susie said,
"We don't need to feel blue.
Let's be **proud** of second place –
that's still special, too."

RIDING SCHOOL

It's still a great trophy!

Susie learned that friends come **first**;
they share the lows and highs.

And **friendship**, not the Glitter Games,
was her very greatest **prize**.